THE LEGEND Of SAM TATE

The Legend of SAM TATE

The character SAM TATE is fictitious and the only resemblance to persons living or dead is purely coincidental. In these stories regarding his legendary status, SAM TATE represents the many thousands of Black Cowboys of the old west and their untold stories. From time to time I refer to documented history concerning actual events which are on record about the history of the west through various genres. However, all events described in the books of SAM TATE are entirely fictitious. This includes supporting characters, names, likenesses, etc. The Legend of SAM TATE is meant to entertain, educate and represent the Black Men and Women of the old west...

Jackie Jonathan Robinson

Author: Jackie Jonathan Robinson
Illustrator: Jackie Jonathan Robinson
Edited By: Tina Lovette Douglas
© Copyright 2016
ISBN: 978-0-9998313-0-4

Grace Throne Productions LLC

In 1868:

U.S. Fourteenth Amendment giving Civil Rights to blacks is ratified. Georgia under military government after legislature expels blacks.

In the 1870's:

During the years after the Civil War, history was made in many of the western states...the names of many outlaws came out; Jesse James, the Younger Brothers...It also gave birth to another breed of men...The Gunfighter! Men like Kingfisher, Wes Hardin, Pat Garett, Billy the Kid and a name never spoken, seemly almost forgotten, a black man who rode angrily through Arizona, New Mexico, Kansas, Wyoming, Montana, and Texas...His was the story that history calls, The Legend of SAM TATE!

The scream echoed within the canyon walls... followed by two gun shots...

The fury in Sam Tate bursted like a stick of Dynamite! He punched Heck Penn and went for his gun... The cabin was very still...

HURRY UP BURN TH' HOUSE, BURN EVERYTHING!

DAMN! HECK CAN'T HANDLE THA' BOY!

MARTY I GOT TH' FOOD

WHOP

EEEEEK!

BDOW

BOOW

BDOW

Sam Tate picked up the handgun he felt the cold iron in his hand the rage... shook his body and hand

Inside the cabin... Frank Logan stood over Amy Tate's lifeless body and cried not because she was dead ...But because she had cut his youthful face... and rejected his advances... outside Sam Tate took cover behind some logs.

ALL YOU HAD TO DO WAS TREAT ME NICE... BUT NO YOU HAD TO CUT MY FACE you.... BLACK o#tunez OF A WOMAN YOU CUT MY FACE!

Legend has it that Sam Tate fought like a mad man that day. A man driven by anger... with the need to destroy or be destroyed himself, the men became one being which he saw with hatered, desperados.

BOOW

BDOW

BDOW

G.HAAA

PWINNGG!

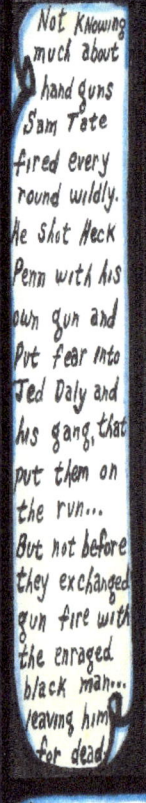

Not Knowing much about hand guns Sam Tate fired every round wildly. He shot Heck Penn with his own gun and put fear into Jed Daly and his gang, that put them on the run... But not before they exchanged gun fire with the enraged black man... leaving him for dead.

ZING
ZING
WIP
ZING

Sam Tate's body, didn't die that day, but something inside of him did; all the goodness and grace toward mankind burned with his house and died with Amy...

HOLD ON THERE MULE...SOME BODY'S MOVING OUT THERE

SOB... AMY... AMY... SOB...SOB

Coming down from the mountains on that day was an old man called "Bear cat Smith"

"BEAR CAT SMITH"

Legend has it that old "Bearcat" doctored Sam Tate, more dead than alive back to hearth, digging three bullets out of him.

IT'S A DAMN SHAME BURN HIS HOME...MURDER HIS WIFE LEAVE HIM FOR DEAD OR TO DIE! DAMN DOGS...NOT MEN...NO HEART...IT'S ENOUGH MAKE YOU SICK!

Amy....Amy

DON'T WORRY FELLA, I'M GOING TO PATCH YOU UP... AND HELP YOU IN SOME WAY... EVEN TEACH YOU TO KILL! GOD FORGIVE ME...

WHO'S YO'... WHERE AM AH?

EASY FELLA... YOU AIN'T BEEN YOUR SELF THIS PAST WEEK...

The rest of the legend tells how "Bearcat Smith" made an empty grave and told Sam Tate his wife was resting there in eternal glory... the mountainman never told Sam how his wife was burned with the house!

AMY! AH' SWEAR BY ALL THA' WE KNOW'D 'BOUT TH' LAWD... THIS NIGHT... THA' AH' WILL NOT REST UNTIL AH' FIND THEM MEN... AH KILL THEM ALL!

AMY MAE TATE

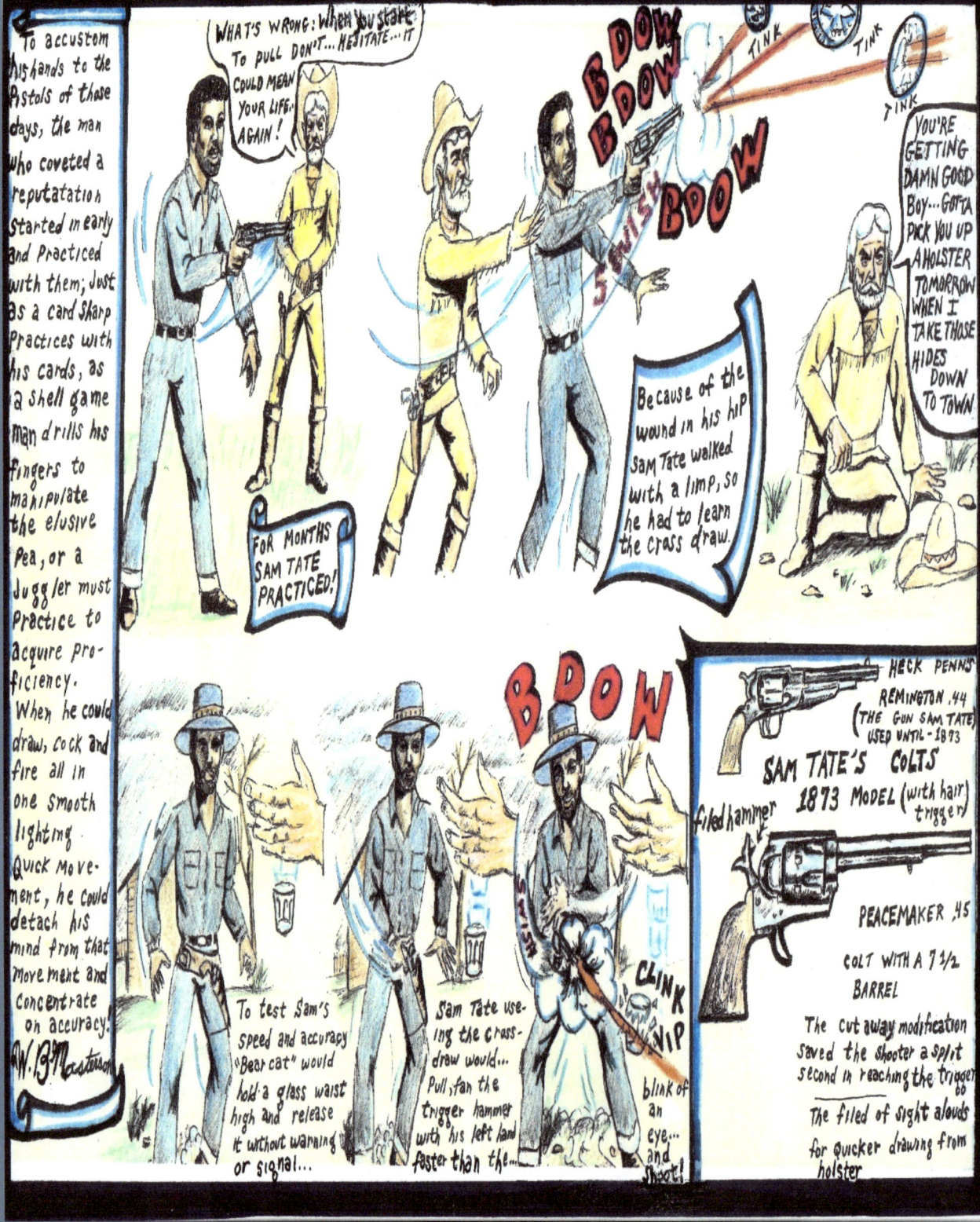

THE LEGENDARY
SAM TATE

Once a runaway Slave, once a Union Soldier, a Widower, a Bounty Hunter, a Law-man, Gambler and Gunfighter. He was but one of the many blacks who help make DODGE CITY, TOMBSTONE, ABILENE and many of the towns and cities of the Old West!

The Saga Continues…

Note:

*In Tribute to John Barrett, a Black Deputy Marshal murdered by the Rufus Buck Gang in 1895...Also Bass Reaves, a Black Deputy Sheriff who served the court of Judge Parker at Fort Smith...

*The Black West
 by William Loren Katz

THE LEGEND Of SAM TATE

"There's a New Sheriff in Town"

Written and Illustrated by Jackie Jonathan Robinson

The legend of Sam Tate had many tales like the time in 1879 when Judge Isaac Parker "The Hanging Judge" the Justice of Indian Territory pinned a deputy-marshal's badge on him... That was just after the Shoot Out with Fancy Dan Moore down in Texas....

NOTE:
IN TRIBUTE TO JOHN BARRETT, A BLACK DEPUTY MARSHAL, MURDERED BY THE RUFUS BUCK GANG IN 1895... ALSO BASS REAVES, A BLACK DEPUTY SHERIFF WHO SERVED THE COURT OF JUDGE PARKER AT ✳ FORT SMITH....

Cold water creek was a small town that tried to keep law an order.... despite the many outlaws that wandered throught, there was little trouble until one Clint Burnett gunned down a local settler in a saloon brawl....

The presence of a black deputy marshal in Cold water creek was big news... And it begin to worry some of the local residence But the real trouble was yet to come Ketchel one of Wade Dance gang listen at the Saloon

The morning Wade Dance chose... was no different the whether was mild... but the streets of Cold Water creek were empty... The dread of a coming destruction at the hands of feared gunfighters... was in the air

HEY BOY WHAT YOU DO SLEEP OUT HERE ALL NIGHT? YOU SURE TAKE YOUR WORK TO HEART

AIN'T THA' MARSH' AH' SLEPT WITH MUH HOSS AT TH' CORRALS.. AH' JEST GOTTA' POWERFUL TASTE FAR YORE COFFEE THIS MORNIN'

SAM YOU EVER DID THIS BEFORE? I MEAN... I HEARD...

YAS... MARSH' AH' DONE IT B'FORE BUT THA DON'T MAKE IT ANY EASIER... KILLIN' IS STILL KILLIN'

AH' WANT CLINT OUTTA JAIL... GOT THA'...! LET'S RIDE!

WELL BOY..! THIS IS IT! AWRIGHT! SAM! BE CAREFUL!

TH' NAMES SAM! YEAH... YO' TOO!

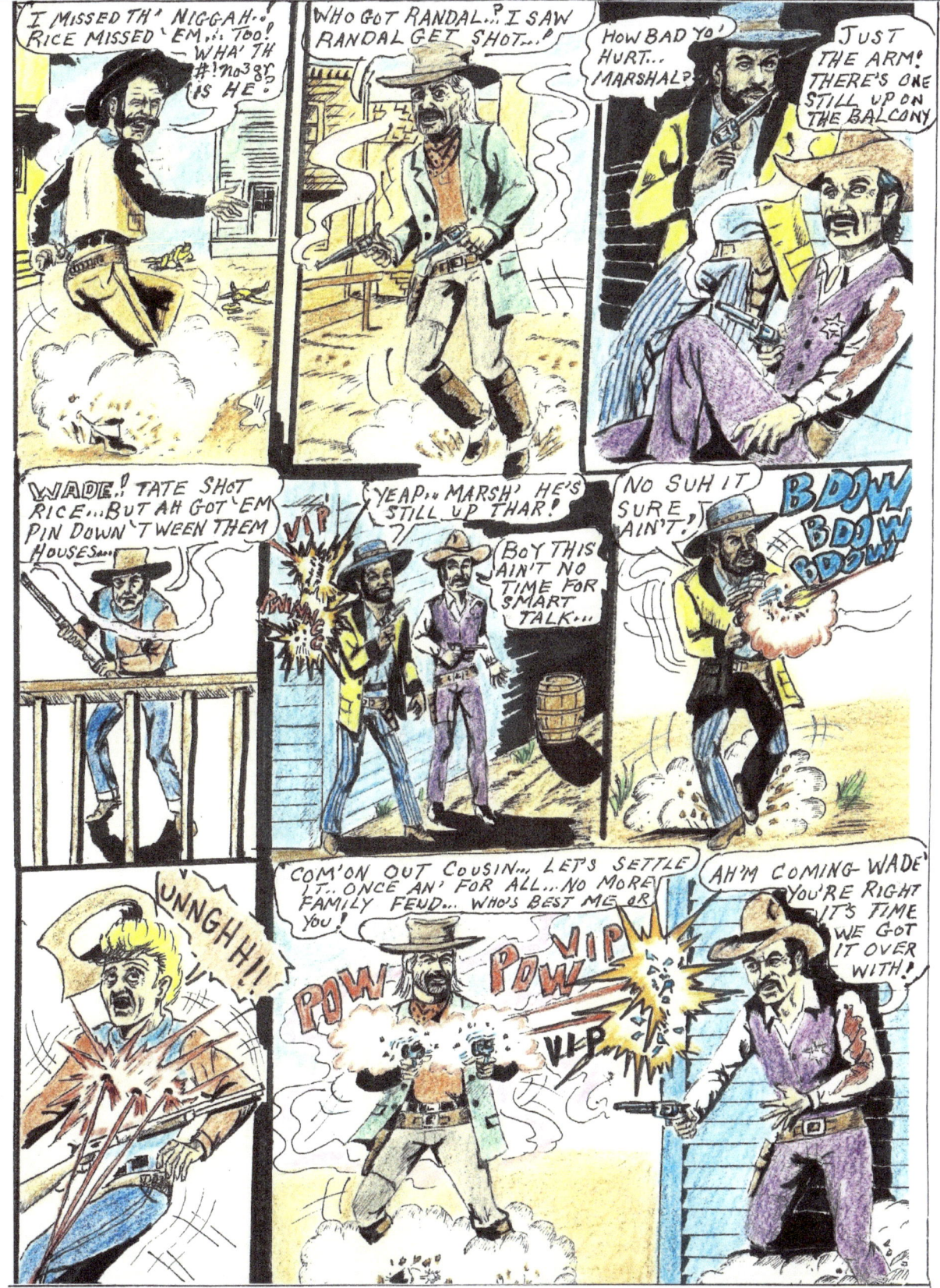

Book 1 Footnotes:

Page 1:
https://www.loc.gov/rr/program/bib/ourdocs/.14thamendme
nt.html#American

Page 3:
https://www.civilwaronthewesternborder.org/encyclopedia/
quantrill-william-clarke

Page 7:
https://www.kansashistory.us/fordco/batmasterson.html

Page 11:
https://www.history.com/this-day-in-history/shootout-at-
the-ok-corral

Page 12:
https://www.smithsonianmag.com/history/stanley-meets-
livingstone-91118102/.

Page 13:
https://www.britannica.com/topic/Atchison-Topeka-and-
Santa-Fe-Railway-Company.

Page 16:
https://www.legendsofamerica.com/nativecivilizedtribes/

THE LEGEND

Spotlight on the Author:

Born and raised in a small town called Winter Haven, Florida; Jackie Jonathan Robinson, an only child traveled to various cities around the US with his Mother (Lorraine). She always made their travel time an adventure for young Jackie. Out of all the places they visited his favorite city was New York. As a young adult he served briefly in the Navy before getting married and fathering three children (Demetri, Tanya and Tina). When the marriage did not work out he relocated to New York where his fourth child (Monique) was born.

While living in New York Jackie experienced one of many seizures and injured himself on the subway. This would lead to many other health issues from that point on. He later contracted tuberculosis in 1984 and was admitted into Harlem Hospital. Unable to totally cure the disease, Harlem Hospital transferred him to the National Jewish Health Hospital in Denver, Colorado. While spending an extensive amount of time in the hospital, Jackie passed the time doing what he was most passionate about, drawing and writing respectively.

It was there in that hospital room in Denver, during his struggle with TB and other ailments that the character "Sam Tate" was born. Over the years as Jackie continued to battle various health challenges he continued expanding the adventures of this character who somehow became the persona of a healthier, more professionally driven version of himself. With each passing year dealing with health crises Jackie found a way to defy the odds and embrace life. His work, his character "Sam Tate" was his life's purpose and he did not mind sharing his books with others.

Sadly, Jackie passed away in October of 2017 after a long battle with Leukemia. Fortunately, he passed on the legacy of his life's work "The Legend of SAM TATE" to his children. We hope that you enjoy the first three books of his creation and hope to share the others soon.

Thank you for your support
The Children of Jackie Jonathan Robinson

of

SAM TATE